Zac and Kat

A Rough Road to Friendship

Written By John & Esther Cooper

Illustrated By Joan Coleman

First Edition: 2021

Library of Congress Control Number 2021911973

ISBN 978-1-7355600-2-1

The authors may be contacted at epcooper39@hotmail.com
EP&J2 PUBLISHING
Crawford, Tennessee

Illustrations by Joan Coleman of Ink Wonderland
www.inkwonderland.com

Dedication

This book is dedicated to our son and daughter-in-law, Jared and Lauryn, of whom we are so very proud, and to our grandchildren, Mac and Rosie, who have brought us great joy.

Acknowledgments

Thank you to our grandchildren, whose vivid imaginations inspired us to write this book.

Judi Heidel at Perfectly Clear Editing Services worked her magic for us again with her patience, superb editing skills, and helpful suggestions.

Joan Coleman of Ink Wonderland brought the words to life with wonderfully enchanting illustrations. Her artwork for the cover and for the interior of the book captured the essence of the characters exactly as we had imagined them.

About the Book

After making many photo books about adventures they have had over the years with their grandchildren, the Coopers decided to publish their first illustrated children's book. While growing up, the Coopers remember people quoting that old adage, "Don't judge a book by its cover." In *Zac and Kat, A Rough Road to Friendship*, it is proven that preconceptions of others are often faulty. If we can rid ourselves of the ingrained social and cultural stigmas, there is the possibility of finding new friends and productive relationships.

About the Authors

Both of the Coopers retired from employment with the Commonwealth of Virginia more than ten years ago. Throughout their years of marriage, they have always enjoyed working together on a variety of projects and can now add publishing a children's book to their list of accomplishments. Having recently sold their mountaintop hideaway in Tennessee, they are looking forward to new adventures, including traveling the country and riding a motorcycle in the desert, as well as spending time with family. The Coopers hope that children and parents alike will gain insight from reading this book. They can be reached via email at epcooper39@hotmail.com.

About the Illustrator

Joan Coleman is a professional artist and book illustrator. She and her husband, Andrew, own and operate Ink Wonderland, an illustration and design company that provides graphic design, illustration, and apparel design services for clients all across the USA.

Zac and Kat

 A Rough Road to Friendship

Rosie's brother Mac had a dog named Zac.

Zac was known for his love of chasing cats.

Mac's sister Rosie had a cat named Kat.

Kat had no patience for a dog like Zac.

Zac chased Kat and caught her by the tail.

Kat turned on Zac and grabbed his tail as well.

This ongoing tussle was not about Zac or Kat,

but rather which pet was better—a dog or a cat.

They rumbled and they tumbled
till they rolled right out the door.

They rolled through a cow pasture

and through a herd of sheep,

disturbing all the residents, who were trying to get some sleep.

They rolled into a farmer's yard, upsetting all his chickens.

A pig eating his morning corn
squealed out, "Hey, what the dickens!"

They rolled through a woodland
and woke an owl from sleep.

The squirrels ran for cover.
Zac and Kat raced toward the creek.

Zac and Kat made a splash, then they disappeared. Zac broke the surface, but Kat did not appear.

Zac dove, found Kat, and dragged her to the shore as cheers went up for Zac, "the dog who saved a cat!"

When Kat had recovered, she and Zac made a pact to be best friends forever and to watch each other's back.

The pact would be their secret since no one would believe that a dog and a cat could live in harmony.

At home Rosie realized there had been a change. She turned to Mac and said, "Those two are acting strange."

They both knew that Zac and Kat had finally come to see there is often more to someone than what we first perceive.

The End

CPSIA information can be obtained
at www.ICGtesting.com
Printed in the USA
LVHW070438270721
693794LV00007B/103

9 781735 5600